Confectious
EASY DESSERTS

Addictively easy-to-make confections that are satisfyingly simple.
—Nicci Julian

PAGE PUBLISHING, INC.
New York, NY

First originally published by Page Publishing, Inc. 2015

ISBN 978-1-68213-883-0 (pbk)
ISBN 978-1-68213-884-7 (digital)

Photos by Max Ross
Instagram: Confectious
Facebook: Nicci Julian

Printed in the United States of America

As you can tell, these desserts will not only be cherished by people.
My English bulldog, Sheila, is a huge lover of anything sweet! She will demand a crumb to fall on the ground with her stubborn attitude until she's satisfied. Clearly these recipes are just too good!

INTRODUCTION

Confectious Desserts was created and inspired by my passion of delicious desserts that are perfect for any time of the year. Addictively easy, delicious, and simple are the words used to describe *Confectious*. *Confectious* is meant to be a resourceful and helpful book that creates happy and memorable experiences through my kitchen to yours. Also, *Confectious* will still have many other subjects as "Easy Desserts" is not the only one. Keep an eye out for the next *Confectious* baking book as I know this book will leave people wanting more of these tasty recipes. As this is the first *Confectious* book to be published, it is only necessary that we celebrate and enjoy with my fabulous cakes, tarts, no-bake desserts, and cookies! Make sure to refer to my resourceful chocolate dipping page if you have any leftover treats.

After attending the Culinary Institute of America in Napa Valley, I started my own company called Custom Cakes by Nicci Cookies and Pies too! Even though I created this small company out of my home in Southern California, it grew fast and became known to everyone through word of mouth. The reason for my fast growing small business was because of my delicious catered desserts and my passion for presentation. Also, after attending the Culinary Institute of America, I attended my internship at the Pelican Hill Resort in Newport Beach, California, where I gained even more knowledge and a greater appreciation for baking. These experiences have influenced my creations for my amazing and simple desserts.

I have created a baking book that makes professional desserts, which can be made by anyone. The recipes in this book have been altered for any beginning or advanced baker as these are recipes that have been created in my home kitchen since I started baking at the age of six. Some of these recipes have been passed down, and others have been inspired from traveling, school, and or work experiences. I hope you find *Confectious* "Easy Desserts" to be delicious, fun, and a resourceful book that guides you through your love for sweets.

My pointer for you is to...

Make life easy... eat dessert first!

To my loving mother, Vallie Julian, my number one supporter

CONFECTIOUS

Cakes

IRRESISTIBLE VANILLA VELVET CAKE WITH RASPBERRY FILLING

Serves 10 to 12

This Vanilla Velvet cake is the perfect cake for any birthdays or family celebrations. This is my second most popular cake that my customers beg for. This cake can also be transformed with any choice of your favorite filling (raspberry, lemon curd, or chocolate fudge). May this life-saving recipe bring you relaxed and joyful memories.

---

1 ½ sticks soft unsalted butter	1 tablespoon white distilled vinegar
½ cup vegetable oil	1 tablespoon vanilla extract
2 cups of granulated sugar	2 ½ cup all-purpose flour
3 large eggs	1 ½ teaspoon baking soda
1 cup buttermilk	½ teaspoon salt
½ cup sour cream or plain yogurt	

- Preheat the oven to 350 degrees and grease 2 eight-inch baking pans.
1. Cream the butter, oil, and sugar together for 2 minutes in a stand mixer fitted with a paddle attachment.
2. Add 3 large eggs one at a time, until fully incorporated.
3. Slightly whisk the buttermilk, sour cream, vinegar, and vanilla in a small bowl and add to the egg and sugar mixture. Then, turn the mixer on medium speed to incorporate. (The mixture will curdle, don't worry!)
4. In a small bowl, whisk the flour, baking soda, and salt together. Then, with the mixer on, slowly add the dry ingredients. Slowly increase the speed to medium until fully incorporated (30 seconds).
5. Lastly, pour the batter evenly into prepared pans and bake for 25 to 30 minutes or until the top is slightly golden brown. Allow to cool.

Vanilla Frosting

1 ½ cups (3 sticks) soft unsalted butter	3 tablespoons of heavy cream
1 ½ teaspoon vanilla extract	3 tablespoons milk
2 ½ pounds of confectioner's sugar	

1. In a stand mixer fitted with a paddle attachment, beat the butter, vanilla, and sugar until completely incorporated.
2. Slowly add the cream and milk until desired consistency.

Raspberry Filling

¾ cup vanilla frosting	1 teaspoon lemon zest
2 tablespoons raspberry jam	¼ cup fresh raspberries

1. Slowly beat ¾ cup of the vanilla frosting with the raspberry jam, lemon zest, and fresh raspberries until combined.
2. Fill the cake layers with the raspberry filling and then ice the cake using an offset spatula.

CLASSY COCONUT CUPCAKES

Makes 24 cupcakes

These sinful coconut cupcakes will melt in your mouth as they are sophisticated and tasteful to the eye. This recipe uses a fluffy vanilla cupcake batter that consists of vanilla, almond extract, and flaked coconut, which is topped with a mouthwatering coconut cream cheese frosting. These cupcakes are delicious, gorgeous, and elegant.

Coconut Cupcakes

1 ½ stick or ¾ cup unsalted butter, softened

1 ½ cup granulated sugar

3 large eggs

2 teaspoons vanilla extract

1 teaspoon almond extract

1 ¼ cup sour cream

2 ½ cup all-purpose flour

1 teaspoon baking powder

½ teaspoon baking soda

½ teaspoon salt

1 ¼ cup sweetened shredded coconut

• Preheat the oven to 350 degrees and prepare two 1 dozen cupcake pans.
1. In a stand mixer fitted with the paddle attachment, beat the sugar and butter together for one minute.
2. Add the eggs one at a time and then the vanilla, almond extract, and sour cream to the mixer.
3. In a small bowl, whisk the dry ingredients together and add to the mixer stirring until combined.
4. Lastly, fold in the coconut.
5. Turn the mixer off and scrape down the bowl until all ingredients are fully incorporated.
6. Fill the cupcake liners 2/3 full using an ice cream scoop and bake for 15 minutes or until fully baked in the center. Set aside to cool before icing.

Cream Cheese Icing

2 cups cream cheese softened

1 ½ cup soft unsalted butter

2 cups +2 tablespoon confectioner's sugar

1 teaspoon vanilla extract

½ teaspoon almond extract

4 cups sweetened shredded coconut

1. Once the cupcakes are cooled, you can beat the cream cheese, butter, confectioner's sugar, vanilla, and almond with a stand mixer fitted with a paddle attachment. Beat until incorporated and frost with an offset spatula or knife. Lastly, dunk the cupcakes in a snowy pile of the shredded coconut.

FANTASTIC FUNFETTI CUPCAKES

Makes 24 Cupcakes

These fluffy and fun funfetti cupcakes couldn't be any easier as they are so delicious! These cupcakes are a vanilla cupcake base filled with bright funfetti sprinkles and topped with a delicious vanilla frosting. Celebrate your next birthday in the sweetest way possible with these fun funfetti cupcakes.

Funfetti Cupcakes

1 ½ stick or ¾ cup unsalted butter, softened

1 ½ cup granulated sugar

3 large eggs

2 teaspoons vanilla extract

½ teaspoon almond extract

1 ¼ cup sour cream

2 ½ cup all-purpose flour

1 teaspoon baking powder

½ teaspoon baking soda

½ teaspoon salt

¾ cup rainbow sprinkles

- Preheat the oven to 350 degrees and prepare two 1 dozen cupcake pans.
1. In a stand mixer fitted with the paddle attachment, beat the sugar and butter together for one minute.
2. Add the eggs one at a time and then the vanilla, almond extract, and sour cream to the mixer.
3. In a small bowl, whisk the dry ingredients together and add to the mixer stirring until combined.
4. Lastly, fold in the sprinkles.
5. Turn the mixer off and scrape down the bowl until all ingredients are fully incorporated.
6. Fill the cupcake liners 2/3 full using an ice cream scoop and bake for 15 minutes or until fully baked in the center. Set aside to cool before icing.

Vanilla Frosting

4 sticks or 2 cups unsalted butter, softened

5 cups powdered sugar

½ tablespoon vanilla extract

1 tablespoon heavy cream

pinch of salt

1 cup rainbow sprinkles (decoration)

1. In a stand mixer fitted with the paddle attachment, beat the butter, sugar, vanilla, and salt together until it comes together.
2. Lastly, add the heavy cream. You may add an extra tablespoon or two if you wish for the frosting to be smoother and not as thick.
3. Ice the cooled cupcakes and decorate with rainbow sprinkles.

DEVINE RED VELVET CUPCAKES WITH CREAM CHEESE ICING

Makes 14 to 15 Cupcakes

This red velvet cupcake recipe is not only moist, but has a rich buttery flavor because it uses butter instead of oil. I have used this recipe for birthday parties, family gatherings, and even for myself. The effortless depth of flavor these cupcakes bring will leave you with a recipe you have for a lifetime.

¾ cup soft unsalted butter
1 cup + 2 tablespoons granulated sugar
2 large eggs
1 1/3 cup all-purpose flour
3 tablespoon cocoa powder
½ teaspoon baking soda
pinch of salt
½ cup buttermilk
1 teaspoon distilled white vinegar
1 tablespoon red food coloring (desired color)
2 teaspoon vanilla extract

- Preheat the oven to 350 degrees and line or grease the cupcake tin.
1. Beat the butter and sugar in a stand mixer fitted with the paddle attachment for 2 minutes.
2. Add one egg at a time to the mixer and beat until incorporated.
3. Whisk the flour, baking soda, and salt together. Measure the buttermilk, vinegar, vanilla, and food coloring together.
4. Add ½ of the dry ingredients to the mixer and while slowly stirring, add all of the wet ingredients. Lastly, add the rest of the flour mixture and stir until incorporated.
5. Fill the cupcake liners 2/3 full using an ice cream scoop. Bakes for 15 to 18 minutes or until the middle of the cupcakes are completely baked. Allow to cool before frosting the cupcakes.

Cream Cheese Icing
2 cups cream cheese softened
1 ½ cup soft unsalted butter
2 cup + 2 tablespoon confectioner's sugar
1 teaspoon vanilla extract
½ teaspoon almond extract

1. Beat the cream cheese, butter, confectioner's sugar, and extracts together on low speed fitted with the paddle attachments. Slowly increase the speed until all ingredients are fully incorporated.
2. Ice the cupcakes with an offset spatula or a butter knife.

GERMAN CHOCOLATE SHEET CAKE

Serves 10 to 12

This easy moist chocolate sheet cake will always be a crowd pleaser as it is known to be "the best chocolate cake ever." This is the most popular cake in my bakery! This cake has a few extra steps than any other recipe in this book, but it is definitely worth it. This rich chocolate cake and irresistible German frosting can also be transformed into cupcakes, round cakes, or jelly roles as this is a sponge cake. I promise once you have made this recipe, you will never make another chocolate cake again.

¾ cup semisweet chocolate chips, melted
4 tablespoons Special Dark Hershey's Cocoa powder
½ cup hot water
12 tablespoons soft unsalted butter
4 large eggs
2 egg yolks
1 cup granulated sugar

1 tablespoon vanilla extract
½ cup sour cream or plain yogurt
½ cup milk
1 ¾ all-purpose flour
1 ½ teaspoon baking soda
½ teaspoon salt

- Preheat the oven to 350 degrees and grease a one 3x9-sheet pan.
1. In a small bowl, combine the hot water with the cocoa powder. Then stir in the melted chocolate chips. Allow to cool slightly for a couple of minutes. Lastly, combine the softened butter and mix until completely combined. Set aside.
2. In a mixer fitted with the whisk attachment, add the eggs, egg yolks, and sugar and whisk on high speed for 5 minutes or until the eggs are pale and have doubled in size.
3. Add the chocolate mixer into the stand mixer with the eggs and beat until incorporated.
4. Then, in a small bowl, whisk the flour, baking soda, and salt together. Then, measure the buttermilk, sour cream, and vanilla.
5. Lastly, add half of the flour mixture to the mixer and stir. While stirring, pour all the wet ingredients into the mixer. Lastly, add the last half of the flour mixture and stir until combined. Scrape down the bowl.
6. Pour evenly into the prepared pan and bake for 18 to 22 minutes. Allow to cool.

German Frosting

1 ½ sticks unsalted butter
1 14-ounce can sweetened condensed milk
1 cup brown sugar
4 large egg yolks
1 ½ teaspoon vanilla extract

¼ teaspoon almond extract
1 ¾ cup sweetened flaked coconut
¾ cup blanched almonds
pinch of salt

1. In a saucepan over medium heat, melt the butter and whisk in the milk, brown sugar, and egg yolks. Bring to a simmer and continue to stir until thickened, about 8 to 10 minutes. Off the heat, add the vanilla extract, almond extract, salt, coconut, and blanched almonds. Allow to cool one hour before frosting the cake.
2. Once the frosting is cooled, pour over the sheet cake and spread with a knife. Drizzle melted chocolate over the top for a gorgeous presentation!

OUTRAGEOUS CHOCOLATE FUDGE DIPPED CUPCAKES

Makes 28 Cupcakes

These cupcakes can be made by the previous chocolate cake recipe but are then dipped in the richest silkiest fudge icing. The cupcakes are dipped in warm fudge and then allowed to rest at room temperature as the fudge will harden but still have a rich and smooth texture. These cupcakes are easy to make for a crowd of chocolate lovers because the process of dipping the cupcakes instead of icing them is so incredibly easy. No fuss or worry, and they come out perfect every time. The ease and simplicity of this recipe will leave you amazed.

Chocolate Cake
Recipe of the chocolate cake can be seen on the previous page.

Chocolate Fudge
½ cup granulated sugar
½ cup heavy cream
1 tablespoon Hershey's Special Dark Cocoa powder
1 cup semisweet chocolate chips
4 tablespoons unsalted butter
1 ½ cup powdered sugar, sifted

1. Scoop the chocolate cake batter into prepared cupcake liners, filling them almost completely to the top. Bake the chocolate cupcakes at 350 degrees for 13 to 16 minutes or until fully baked in the middle.
2. In a microwavable bowl, combine the sugar and heavy cream together. Microwave for 1 minute or until the cream is very hot.
3. Pour the cream mixture over a bowl of cocoa powder, chocolate chips, and butter.
4. Stir until melted and set over a pot of simmering water if it is not completely melted.
5. Sift the powdered sugar over the chocolate mixture and stir until combined.
6. Lastly, dip and gently lift the cupcake out of the warm fudge or use a spoon to spread the fudge over the cupcakes. Allow to cool and decorate with chocolate shavings.

"PIECE OF CAKE" CARROT CAKE WITH CREAM CHEESE ICING

Serves 10 to 12

This carrot cake recipe is the moistest and most flavorful cake you will ever have. Since it contains oil and freshly grated carrots, the texture is lightly, fluffy, and moist. Feel free to add raisins or pineapple since that is traditional in many carrot cake recipes However, the crunch from the walnuts along with the smooth and rich cream cheese frosting is decadent as is. Enjoy this absolutely divine carrot cake.

1 cup vegetable oil
2 cups granulated sugar
1 tablespoon vanilla extract
3 cups shredded carrots
4 large eggs
2 cups all-purpose flour
2 teaspoons baking soda
2 teaspoons baking powder
1 teaspoon ground cinnamon
1 teaspoon salt
1 cup lightly chopped walnuts

- Preheat the oven to 350 degrees and grease two 8-inch baking pans.
1. In a stand mixer fitted with the paddle attachment, beat the oil, sugar, vanilla, and shredded carrots (shred your carrots in a food processor or a cheese grater) for 3 minutes.
2. Then, add the four eggs one at a time.
3. Lastly, add the dry ingredients and stir until fully incorporated. Then, fold in the slightly chopped walnuts.
4. Bake for 25 to 30 minutes or until golden brown.

Cream Cheese Icing
2 cups cream cheese, softened
1 ½ cup unsalted butter, softened
2 cups +2 tablespoons confectioner's sugar
1 teaspoon vanilla extract

1. Beat the cream cheese, butter, confectioner's sugar, and vanilla together on low speed fitted with the paddle attachments. Slowly increase the speed and add a splash of orange juice until you have the desired consistency and all ingredients are fully incorporated. Ice the cake using an offset spatula or a large cake carving knife (as the cooks traditionally did in the restaurant).

CLASSIC BANANA CAKE WITH HONEY CREAM CHEESE FROSTING

Serves 10 to 12

My banana cake with honey cream cheese frosting is light, bright, and flavorful with all of the amazing textures from the moist cake to the smooth and airy frosting. This moist banana cake is a perfect complement to the amazing honey cream cheese frosting since the banana cake is not overly sweet. This cake will become very popular at any birthday or holiday celebrations. Enjoy this incredibly blissful cake.

Banana Cake

3 ripe bananas
¾ cup granulated sugar
½ cup brown sugar
½ cup vegetable oil
2 large eggs
¼ teaspoon ground cinnamon
¼ cup sour cream or plain yogurt
¼ cup buttermilk

2 teaspoons vanilla extract
1 teaspoon orange zest
2 cups all-purpose flour
1 teaspoon baking soda
¼ teaspoon salt
½ cup chopped walnuts
1 6 ounce bag walnut, finely chopped for decorating

- Preheat the oven to 350 degrease and grease two 8-inch baking pans.
1. In a stand mixer fitted with a paddle attachment, mash the ripe bananas.
2. In the same bowl, mix the mashed bananas, sugar, oil, eggs, cinnamon, sour cream, vanilla, and orange zest.
3. Then, add the flour, baking soda, salt, and walnuts. Mix until completely incorporated.
4. Pour batter into the prepared pans and bake for 35 to 40 minutes or until golden brown and baked through the center of the cakes.

Honey Cream Cheese Frosting

2 cups cream cheese, softened
1 ½ cup unsalted butter, softened
1 cup powdered sugar
4 tablespoons honey
½ teaspoon orange zest

1. In a stand mixer fitted with a paddle attachment, beat the cream cheese, butter, sugar, honey, and orange zest together until smooth.
2. Ice and fill the cake using an offset spatula or knife. Decorate with the chopped walnuts around the cake.

BEST BANANA CHOCOLATE CHIP BREAD

Serves 6 to 8

As if my banana cake with honey cream cheese frosting wasn't enough, my banana choco-late chip bread completes the banana cake extravaganza. The combination of banana and choc-olate is the reason why this bread is the best. Flavorful, moist, sweet, and best served with a cup of coffee or as a midnight craving. Enjoy this simple and indulging treat with fam-ily and friends as it will soon be known as their best banana chocolate chip bread recipe.

½ cup or 1 stick unsalted butter, softened

1 cup granulated sugar

2 large eggs

2 ½ or 1 cup ripe bananas

½ cup sour cream

1 teaspoon vanilla extract

1 ½ cups all-purpose flour

1 teaspoon baking soda

1 teaspoon salt

¾ cup mini semisweet chocolate chips

- Preheat the oven to 350 degrees and grease a 9-by-5-by 3-inch loaf pan (normal loaf pan size).
1. In a stand mixer fitted with a paddle attachment, beat the butter and sugar for 2 minutes.
2. Add the eggs one at a time and scrape down the bowl.
3. Then, add the mashed ripe bananas, sour cream, and vanilla together.
4. Lastly, add the dry ingredients and stir until incorporated. Fold in the chocolate chips.
5. Pour the batter into the prepared pan and bake for 50 minutes to 1 hour or until golden brown and not jiggling in the middle. Allow to cool slightly before removing from the loaf pan and cutting.

GAM GAM'S EASY LEMON CAKE

Serves 12 to 15

This fresh and vibrant lemon cake has been the centerpiece of many holiday gatherings. Grandma Marie or Gam Gam has created the perfect recipe for a bright and lemony dessert no one can resist. This easy to make cake is baked in a presentable dish and then drenched with a lemon icing and served as is. Simple, sinful, and stunning.

1 yellow cake mix
1 small lemon Jell-O packet
¾ cup water
¾ cup vegetable oil
4 large eggs

- Preheat the Oven to 325 degrees and grease a 9x13 baking pan.
1. In a bowl, whisk together the yellow cake mix, Jell-O packet, water, oil, and eggs until smooth.
2. Pour the batter in a greased baking dish and bake for forty-five to sixty minutes or until golden brown.

Lemon Glaze

2 cups confectioner's sugar
zest from 2 lemons
juice from 2 lemons

1. In a bowl, whisk together the sugar, lemon zest, and lemon juice until smooth.
2. Once the cake is baked, poke holes in the top of the cake while still warm.
3. Pour the glaze on top of the cake and allow to cool or refrigerate before serving.

SCRUMPTIOUS STRAWBERRY SHORTCAKE TRIFLE

Serves 4 to 6

My version of strawberry shortcake has always been large mounds of buttery biscuits that are similar to a moist scone, along with a lot of fresh strawberries and their juice, and accompanied by white clouds of fresh whip cream. This dessert cannot only be altered in size for special events, but can also be assembled at the last minute. The best way to serve this dessert is in a trifle dish because it is not only stunning but also incredibly easy to prepare for family and large crowds. The fresh and natural flavors of this dessert will leave your family, neighbors, and guests begging all year round.

Biscuit Dough

1 cup all-purpose flour
2 teaspoons baking powder
¼ teaspoon salt
2 tablespoons granulated sugar
3 tablespoon unsalted butter, cut into cubes
¼ cup + 1 tablespoon cream
1 large egg

- Preheat the oven to 375 degrees and lightly grease a baking sheet.
1. In a mixer fitted with a paddle attachment, stir the flour, baking powder, salt, and sugar together.
2. Add the diced cold butter and stir until the butter looks like small peas.
3. Lightly beat the egg and cream together and add to the mixer just until combined.
4. Knead the dough on a floured work surface just until it comes together (10 seconds, that's it!).
5. Roll out the dough and cut into small circles using a biscuit cutter.
6. Bake for 13 to 15 minutes or until fluffy and lightly golden brown. Set aside to cool.

Strawberry and Sauce

2 pints fresh strawberries, cut in quarters
2 tablespoons granulated sugar
Juice of 1 lemon

1. In a bowl, mix the strawberries, sugar, and lemon together. Set aside in a refrigerator for at least 1 hour before assembling.

Fresh Whip Cream

2 cups heavy whipping cream
½ cup powdered sugar
1 teaspoon vanilla extract

1. Before serving, break the biscuits apart and place in the bottom of the trifle dish. Then, put a layer of the fresh strawberries and their juice on top of the biscuits. Lastly, spread the whip cream onto of the strawberries. Repeat the process until finished.

THE ULTIMATE CINNAMON BUNDT CAKE

Serves 8 to 10

Cinnamon Bundt Cake is an easy cake recipe that replicates the flavors of a cinnamon roll. This recipe is so incredibly easy as it is baked using a simple cake box mix and swirled with a decadent cinnamon filling. This cake is then baked off in a Bundt cake pan and best served warm with a cup of coffee. The aroma of the baked cinnamon along with the creamy glaze will leave your guests speechless and craving for more.

Cake Base

115.25 ounce vanilla cake box
3 large eggs
½ cup vegetable oil
1/3 cup sour cream
2/3 cup milk

- Preheat the oven to 350 degrees and grease a normal-size Bundt cake pan.
1. In a large mixing bowl, whisk together the wet ingredients.
2. Add the wet ingredients to the dry cake box mix and whisk until combined.
3. Pour batter into the prepared baking dish and set aside as you make the swirled filling.

Cinnamon Swirl filling

1 cup unsalted butter, softened
½ cup brown sugar
1 ½ tablespoon ground cinnamon
1 teaspoon vanilla extract

1. In a mixing bowl, stir together the butter, sugar, cinnamon, and vanilla until combined.
2. Scoop spoonful of the topping over the batter.
3. Using a knife, swirl the topping through the batter.
4. Bake the cake for 35 to 40 minutes or until golden brown on the edges.

Vanilla Glaze

1 cup powdered sugar
3 tablespoons heavy cream
1 tablespoon unsalted butter, melted

1. Whisk the powdered sugar, cream, and melted butter together.
2. Pour the glaze over the warm cake and serve using a large spoon or spatula.

Pies / Cobblers / Tarts / Bars

SWEET AND SIMPLE STRAWBERRY PIE

Serves 10 to 12

My amazing sweet and simple strawberry pie was inspired by my love for the beautiful strawberry season. Even if strawberries aren't in season, this pie could be used with frozen strawberries that have a little extra sugar added to them. What makes this pie so easy is the store-bought piecrust that is baked by itself and drenched with fresh sweet strawberries that is then topped with a gorgeous mound of fresh whip cream. Enjoy this finger-licking pie.

Pie Crust

Store-Bought Pie Crust, Frozen and Thawed

- Preheat the oven to 350 degrees and set aside a 9-inch pie dish
1. Roll out the thawed piecrust, and using your rolling pin, place the piecrust over the pie dish.
2. Place something heavy over the piecrust during baking such as another pie dish or lay down a sheet of foil that has dried beans over the top. This will allow the piecrust not to puff up during baking.
3. Bake the piecrust for 15 to 18 minutes or until golden brown around the edges.

Strawberry Filling

5 cups fresh or frozen strawberries, cut into quarters
1 cup powdered sugar
½ teaspoon lemon zest
Juice from ½ lemon
pinch of salt

1. While the piecrust is baking, you may start to make the strawberry filing by placing the cut strawberries in a bowl.
2. Lastly, mix the sugar, lemon zest, lemon juice, and salt together. Set aside in the refrigerator for 20 minutes.
3. Once the pie is baked and cooled, add the fresh strawberries and their juice. Set aside while you make the fresh whipped cream.

Fresh Whip Cream

1 cup whipping cream
½ cup powdered sugar
1 teaspoon vanilla extract
1 tablespoon mint, chopped

1. In a stand mixer fitted with the whisk attachment, add the cream, sugar, and vanilla to the bowl.
2. Start the mixer on low and slowly increase to high as the cream thickens (4 to 5 minutes).
3. Once the cream is finished, use an offset spatula or rubber spatula to top off the strawberry pie. Decorate with chopped mint for a gorgeous presentation and allow to chill for one hour before serving.

TRADITIONAL BLUEBERRY BLACKBERRY COBBLER

Serves 10 to 12

This Blueberry Blackberry Cobbler was inspired by my teachings at the Pelican Hill Resort in Newport Beach, California. I learned how to make their version of a peach cobbler, but later went home and discovered my own twist on the perfect Blueberry Blackberry Cobbler. This traditional Blueberry Blackberry Cobbler has an almond infused cake bottom with a bright blueberry, blackberry filling, along with a crumble topping. This family style dessert will leave you desiring more.

Cobbler Bottom

¼ cup shortening or unsalted butter, softened
1 cup granulated sugar
1 teaspoon almond extract
1 cup warm whole milk

1 ½ cup all-purpose flour
½ tablespoon baking powder
½ teaspoon salt

- Preheat the oven to 350 degrees and grease a large baking dish of your choice.
1. In a stand mixer fitted with a paddle attachment, beat the shortening, sugar, and almond extract for 2 minutes.
2. Then, warm the milk in the microwave until it is lukewarm and won't completely melt the butter in the mixer. Once lukewarm, add to the mixer and continue to stir.
3. Whisk the flour, baking powder, and salt together and add completely to the mixer. Continue to stir till smooth (30 seconds). Allow to cool completely in the refrigerator for 45 minutes. Once chilled, pour the batter into the greased baking dish and set aside.

Crumble Topping

1 teaspoon vanilla extract
3 tablespoons melted unsalted butter
½ cup +1 tablespoon all-purpose flour

¼ cup granulated sugar
½ teaspoon ground cinnamon
pinch of salt

1. In a saucepan, melt the butter and add the flour, sugar, cinnamon, salt, and vanilla extract. Stir till crumbly and combined. Refrigerate until cool and then sprinkle over the blueberries 15 minutes before the cobbler is finished baking.

Blueberry/Blackberry Filling

3 cups fresh blueberries
2 cups fresh blackberries
½ cup granulated sugar

¼ cup brown sugar
juice of one lemon

zest of 1 lemon
½ teaspoon salt

1. In a large bowl, combine the blueberries, sugars, lemon juice, zest, and salt. Pour the blueberries over the cobbler bottom and bake at 350 degrees for 45 to 50 minutes or until the cobbler bottom is completely baked. Sprinkle the crumble topping over the warm blueberries 15 minutes before the cobbler is finished baking.
   - ❖ Each components of this recipe (cobbler bottom, crumble topping, blueberry filling) can be made days or weeks in advanced if stored in a freezer or refrigerator properly. Assemble and bake the day of serving.

MICHELLE'S PEACH CRISP

Serves 4 to 6

My amazing family friend and second mother has made the best peach crisp over the past couple of years for a quick make ahead dessert. She explains her recipe as a "little handful of this" and a "little handful of that." As you can tell, it is a no-fail peach crisp recipe. However, I have created measurements for the best results. Enjoy this fast and relaxed home-style dessert!

2 pounds ripe sweet peaches (not mushy), peeled, halved, pitted, and cut into ½ inch thick or frozen and thawed peaches

1/3 cup brown sugar

1 tablespoon granulated sugar

zest of ½ lemon

juice of 1 lemon

4 tablespoon unsalted butter, melted

pinch of salt

- Preheat the oven to 350 degrees and grease four mall ramekins or one large 8x8 baking dish.
1. In a small bowl, combine the peeled, cut, and pitted peaches, sugars, lemon juice, zest, butter, and salt.
2. Place in a greased dish and set aside.

Crumble Topping

3 tablespoons melted unsalted butter

½ cup +1 tablespoon all-purpose flour

¼ cup granulated sugar

½ teaspoon ground cinnamon

½ cup quick-cooking oats

1/3 cup toasted halved almonds

1 teaspoon vanilla extract

pinch of salt

1. In a saucepan, melt the butter and combine the flour, sugar, cinnamon, oats, almonds, vanilla, and salt. Stir till crumbly and combined. Refrigerate until cool and then sprinkle over the peaches. Bake 25 to 30 minutes until golden brown and bubbly.

PRETTY PEAR AND ALMOND CROSTATA

Serves 6 to 8

This time-saving elegant Italian crostata will soon be one of your favorite go to desserts. A crostata is similar to a pie but has no fuss of making a perfect crust as it is known for its naturally rustic presentation. This two-step process of assembling the crostata dough and fruit filling couldn't be easier. Enjoy this incredibly delicious and simple dessert.

Crostata Dough
2 cups all-purpose flour
5 tablespoons granulated sugar
pinch of salt
1 cup unsalted butter, cold
2 tablespoons cold water

- Preheat the oven to 400 degrees and slightly grease a baking sheet.
1. In a stand mixer fitted with the paddle attachment, stir the flour, sugar, and salt.
2. Add the cold-diced butter and stir until the butter is the size of small peas.
3. Slowly incorporate the cold water.
4. Knead the dough on a flowered work surface just until combined and refrigerate for 30 minutes.
5. Roll the dough to an 11-inch circle and transfer to a baking sheet. Store in the refrigerator.

Pear and Almond Filling
1/2 stick almond paste
1 egg white
3 15.25 ounce canned pears, drained
and sliced ½-inch thick
1 tablespoon granulated sugar
1 tablespoon brown sugar

zest of ¼ orange
2 tablespoons unsalted butter, cubed
¼ cup sliced almonds
egg wash (1 egg beaten with a splash of water)
¼ cup apricot jam

1. In a stand mixer fitted with the paddle attachment, beat the almond paste and egg white together until combined, 2 minutes.
2. Then, spread the almond mixture over the crostata dough.
3. Gently add the sliced pears over the dough, creating a pretty design. Assemble the design by placing the pears along the dough in a concentric circle until all of the pears have been used. Then, fold the sides of the dough over the pears to create a rustic presentation.
4. Then, sprinkle the sugars, zest, and butter over the top of the pears.
5. Lastly, brush the sides of the dough with the egg wash and sprinkle over the sliced almonds.
6. Bake for 30 to 35 minutes or until golden brown and brush the apricot jam over the crust and pears. Serve warm.

FLAKEY FRENCH APPLE TART

Serves 6 to 8

My French Apple Tart recipe was inspired by the Culinary Institute of America. As I attended school there, the most challenging concept was learning the French Apple Tart. However, I have converted this recipe to be the easiest most delicious French pastry, with warm and crisp Granny Smith apples anyone could ever make. This dessert can be served warm with a scoop of ice cream, or it can be served at room temperature. Enjoy this painless no-fuss mouthwatering dessert.

Tart Dough
1 package of frozen, thawed puff pastry dough
egg wash (1 beaten egg with a splash of water)

- Preheat the oven to 375 degrees and lightly grease a sheet pan.
1. Roll out the puff pastry on a lightly floured work surface to 14x5 inches or any rectangular shape. Trim off any uneven edges with a sharp knife. Set aside in the refrigerator. (Always keep your puff pastry cold!)

Apple Filling
3 Granny Smith apples, peeled, cored, and cut into ¼-inch thick slices
1 tablespoon sugar
½ tablespoon ground cinnamon
2 tablespoons unsalted butter, melted
1 tablespoon apricot jam

1. Once you have sliced the apples, place them uniformly in an even pattern on the dough.
2. Then, sprinkle the sugar, cinnamon, and melted butter evenly.
3. Lightly brush the puff pastry with the egg wash and allow to cool in the refrigerator for 15 to 20 minutes.
4. Bake for 35 to 40 minutes or until baked all the way through and golden brown.
5. Lastly, for an easy spread, brush the apples and crust with the apricot jam to make a pretty sheen.
   ❖ Scoop vanilla ice cream over warm tart for best results.

LUSCIOUS LEMON MERINGUE TART

Serves 6 (4 small tarts or 1 medium size tart)

My gorgeous lemon meringue tart is made with a few ingredients: buttery crust, bright lemon filling, and topped with smooth white clouds of meringue. This three-step tart is finger-licking good anytime of the year. This tart can be converted into any size, such as mini tarts for a catered event, and it can also be made ahead of time and assembled the last minute. Enjoy this buttery, sweet, and tart dessert all year round!

Tart Shell Dough

1 ¼ + 1 tablespoon all-purpose flour
3 tablespoon granulated sugar
pinch of salt

8 tablespoons unsalted butter, cold
2 tablespoon cold water

- Preheat the oven to 375 degrees and grease a large round or rectangular tart shell pan.
1. In a stand mixer fitted with the paddle attachment, combine the flour, sugar, and salt together.
2. Add the diced cold butter and blend until the butter is the size of peas.
3. Add the cold water until the dough comes together.
4. On a lightly flowered work surface, wrap the dough in plastic wrap and refrigerate for 30 minutes.
5. Once the dough is chilled, roll out into a large round circle or rectangle, depending on the size of your tart pan.
6. *Gently* place the dough into the pan and press the excess dough of the edges. Prick the bottom of the dough with a fork and place foil sheet over the tart filled with dried beans to weigh down the tart during baking. Refrigerate the tart shell for 1 hour before baking.
7. Bake the tart for a total of 30 to 35 minutes and remove the foil halfway through baking. Set aside to cool.

Lemon Filling

3 large egg yolks
zest of 1 lemon
juice of 1 lemon (1/4 cup)

5 tablespoons granulated sugar
pinch of salt

1. In a saucepan over medium heat, whisk together the yolks, sugar, lemon juice, zest, and salt.
2. Continue to whisk until the curd thickens or coats the back of a spoon. (It should be pretty thick). Set aside to cool.
3. Once cooled, fill the tart shell with the lemon curd.

Toasted Meringue

4 large egg whites
¼ teaspoon cream of tartar

½ cup granulated sugar
pinch of salt

1. In a stand mixer fitted with the whisk attachment, whip the egg whites, cream of tartar, sugar, and salt o high speed until thick and stiff peaks form.
2. Pour the meringue over the tart and use a mini blow torch or a hot conventional oven to brown the tips of the meringue.

HEAVENLY CHOCOLATE TART

Serves 8 to 10

My mouthwatering chocolate tart has the perfect combination of a buttery crunchy tart and a smooth silky filling. This tart is quick and easy as there is no effort needed to roll out any dough. Press the chocolate graham cracker crust into the tart shell and bake along with the filling for only 20 minutes. Have an elegant and sophisticated dessert in no time.

Chocolate Graham Cracker Crust

1 cup chocolate graham crackers or chocolate cookies crushed in a large bag or food processor
5 tablespoons unsalted butter, melted
2 teaspoons granulated sugar

- Preheat the oven to 350 degrees and grease a 9-inch round tart pan.

1. In a large bowl, mix the finely crushed chocolate graham crackers, melted butter, and sugar together.
2. Press the mixture into the tart pan and bake for ten minutes or until firm.

Chocolate Filling

2 cups bittersweet chocolate chips
½ stick or ¼ cup unsalted butter, softened
3 large eggs
½ teaspoon almond extract
1 teaspoon vanilla extract
2 tablespoons granulated sugar

1. In a small bowl, melt the chocolate and butter over a pan of simmering water. Stir occasionally until fully melted. Set aside.
2. In a large bowl, whisk the eggs, extract, and sugar together.
3. Whisk the chocolate mixture into the egg mixture until combined.
4. Pour the batter into the tart shell and bake for 20 to 23 minutes or until the chocolate has set, but is still slightly gooey in the center.

MINI RASPBERRY TARTS

Serves 8 to 10

My Mini Raspberry Tarts are a no-bake recipe as the mini shortbread crust is store-bought, but the divine vanilla pastry cream is homemade along with the fresh raspberries dusted with powdered sugar. These mini tarts are perfect for entertaining and couldn't be easier to make. Buy any mini tart shells at your local supermarket and prepare the pastry cream a week in advanced. Assemble last minute and indulge immediately. Gorgeous, simple, and the most delicious treat!

Shortbread Tart Shell
Buy any mini or small shortbread tart shells at your local grocery store.
2 cups fresh raspberries

Vanilla Pastry Cream
1 cup whole milk
1 large egg
2 large egg yolks
1/3 cup granulated sugar
¼ cup cornstarch
pinch of salt
1 teaspoon vanilla extract

1. Pour the milk in a saucepan over medium heat until very hot or simmering.
2. In a mixing bowl, whisk together the eggs, yolks, sugar, and cornstarch for 2 minutes or until pale in color.
3. Slowly whisk the hot milk into the egg mixture and continue to stir.
4. Add the milk and egg mixture back to the saucepan and continue to cook over medium heat until fully thickened. Whisk continuously until thickened (you will know when it thickens).
5. Stir in the vanilla extract and allow to cool completely before filling the tart shells.

Assemble

1. Once the pastry cream is cooled, spoon as much or as little cream into the tarts.
2. Pick three fresh raspberries and place on top of the pastry cream.
3. Lastly, dust with powdered sugar and store in the refrigerator before serving.

PERFECT PECAN BARS

Serves 14 to 16 Small Bars/ 8 Large Bars

These sticky, sweet, gooey pecan bars are the best cure to a sweet tooth. This irresistible cara-melly flavor with a crunchy bight from the pecans replicates a pecan pie, but has the lush butter flavor of a shortbread crust. The simple method of pressing the dough into the pan is the reason why these bars are so easy and fun to make with families. These are truly the best pecan bars.

Short Bread Crust
1 3/4 cup all-purpose flour
3/4 cup unsalted butter, softened
1/3 cup sugar

- Preheat the oven to 350 degrees.
1. In a stand mixer, beat the butter and sugar together. Add the flour until it resembles coarse crumbs.
2. Press the dough into an 8x8 ungreased baking dish and bake for 20 to 22 minutes or until the edges are browned. Take out of the oven and add the pecan pie filling.

Pecan Pie Filling
5 tablespoons unsalted butter
1 cup brown sugar
¾ cup dark corn syrup
2 cups coarsely chopped pecans
pinch of salt
1 teaspoon vanilla extract
2 large eggs, 1 egg yolk

1. In a saucepan, whisk together the butter, sugar, corn syrup, and salt. Allow to come to a boil for 2 minutes.
2. Set aside until lukewarm and whisk the pecans, vanilla, and eggs into the caramel mixture.
3. Pour over the shortbread crust and bake for 35 to 40 minutes or until the sides are bubbly, and it has a slight jiggle in the center when you shake it. Allow to cool before cutting into squares.

FANTASTIC SALTED CARAMEL FUDGE BARS

Serves 6 to 8

My Fantastic Salted Caramel Fudge Bars could be called brownies, but the name does not quiet do justice as these bars are the fuggiest things you will ever try. Not only is there a layer of the fudge cake, but also there is a thin layer of a caramel drizzle sprinkled with sea salt. These sinful bars are any chocolate lovers dream.

Fudge Cake

2 tablespoons unsalted butter	1 cup brown sugar
1 cup all-purpose flour	½ cup yogurt or sour cream
¼ cup unsweetened cocoa powder	¼ cup vegetable oil
¼ teaspoon salt	1 teaspoon vanilla extract
¼ teaspoon baking soda	¾ cup coarsely chopped walnuts
4 large eggs	1 ¼ cup dark chocolate chips or chopped bar

- Preheat the oven to 375 degrees and grease a 9x13 baking dish.
1. Melt the chocolate and butter in a microwave until completely melted (don't burn on high heat).
2. In a separate bowl, mix the flour, cocoa powder, salt, and baking soda.
3. In another separate bowl, whisk together the eggs, sugar, sour cream, oil, and vanilla together.
4. Then, add the wet ingredients to the melted butter and chocolate mixture until smooth.
5. Lastly, add the dry ingredients and fold in the chopped walnuts.
6. Pour into the baking dish and bake for 20 minutes or until still slightly gooey. Allow to cool before icing.

Caramel Drizzle

1 ½ cup granulated sugar
1/3 cup water
1 ¼ cup heavy cream
½ teaspoon vanilla extract
sprinkle sea salt or fleur de sel
sprinkle mini chocolate chips

1. In a saucepan, mix the water and sugar.
2. Over medium-low, melt the sugar mixture for 5 to 8 minutes until completely dissolved. Do not stir at this point!
3. Gently swirl the pan once in a while and turn off the heat once the sugar is a light amber color.
4. Turn off the heat and slowly add the vanilla and heavy cream, whisking vigorously.
5. Turn the heat back on to low and continue to whisk until the mixture comes together in a beautiful sauce (2 minutes). Drizzle sauce, chips, and salt over fudge bars.

BAKED BROWNIE PUDDING

Serves 12

Baked Brownie Pudding is a moist, warm, and decadent dessert that is served warm by itself as it is satisfyingly rich. Not only does this dessert satisfy the needs of all chocolate lovers, but it also has the velvety gooey texture of a pudding that is loved by all. You will become amazed at the little effort needed to make this delectable bake and serve dessert.

2 sticks or 1 cup unsalted butter, melted
1 cup brown sugar
4 large eggs
1 teaspoon vanilla extract
¾ cup Hershey's Special Dark Cocoa Powder
½ cup all-purpose flour
pinch of salt
¾ cup semisweet chocolate chips

- Preheat the oven to 325 degrees and grease a large deep round baking dish (around 2 quarts)
1. In a heatproof bowl, melt the butter in a microwave for 50 seconds and set aside to cool.
2. In a stand mixer fitted with the paddle attachment, whisk the eggs and sugar for 6 to 7 minutes until thickened.
3. Add the vanilla, flour, cocoa powder, and salt to the egg and sugar mixture until combined.
4. With the mixer on low, add the melted butter and chocolate chips until smooth.
5. Pour the batter into the prepared baking dish and bake for 55 minutes to 1 hour or until the edges are cooked and the center remains gooey.

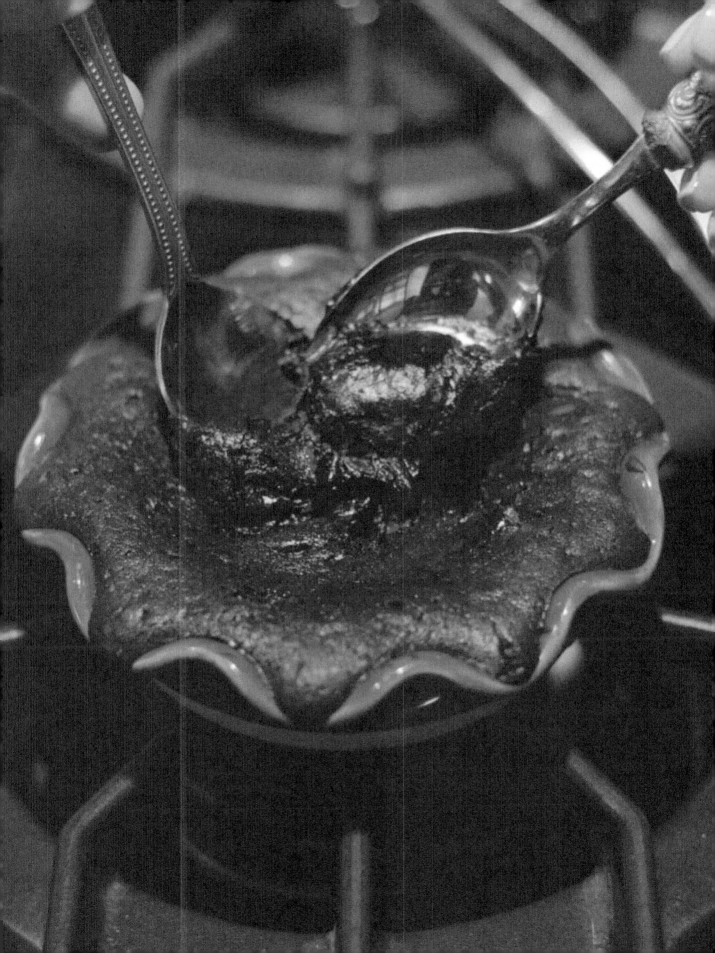

No-Bake Desserts

CHEF MASSIMO'S TIRAMISU

Serves 10

Chef Massimo is a wonderful family friend who has moved from Italy to the United States with his lovely wife, my boyfriend's aunt, Marissa. This lovely couple has a thriving appreciation for food just like myself, so they have opened their own restaurant called Luna Trattoria in Fort Bragg, Northern California, where they only serve authentic Italian style dishes. I am very grateful to share Chef Massimo's killer tiramisu, as it is his mother's recipe. Trust me, you haven't had tiramisu until you've tried Chef Massimo's. I ask for this as a Christmas present and can now gratefully share with all of you. Grazie, Massimo and Marissa.

Tiramisu

2 cups mascarpone, softened

5 large eggs, separated

2/3 cup granulated sugar

1 cup cooled fresh coffee

3 to 4 dozen store-bought lady fingers

1/3 cup Hershey's special dark Cocoa Powder, for dusting

- Have a ½ size pan (12 inches wide) 2 ½ inches deep or medium size trifle dish on hand. However, any square dish will work. Lastly, have a cool pot of fresh coffee ready to be dipped in the ladyfingers.
1. In a mixer fitted with the paddle attachment, whip the egg yolks and sugar on high speed until very thickened, about 5 to 6 minutes.
2. Then, with the mixer starting on high speed, add the softened mascarpone to the egg yolk mixture. Continue to whip for two minutes.
3. In a large bowl, whip the egg whites until firm peaks or until the whites can stand up on the whisk by themselves.
4. Then, using a whisk, gently incorporate the egg yolk and mascarpone mixture to the egg whites until completely combined.

Assemble

1. For the two layers of the tiramisu, arrange half of the soaked ladyfingers in the bottom of the dish. Spread half of mascarpone mixture over ladyfingers, and then dust liberally with the cocoa powder. Repeat the layers until all of the ladyfingers have been used. End with the rest of the mascarpone mixture on top and dust with cocoa powder. Cover and refrigerate for 4 to 6 hours.
- For more layers, use a wider dish.

ADULT CHOCOLATE MOUSE

Serves 6 to 8

This amazing Adult Chocolate Mouse recipe is so versatile as it can be flavored with any liquor of your choice. However, Amaretto liquor has been the most popular between Chambord and Grande Marnier. This dessert is not only simple to make but contains a small amount of ingredients. Simple, elegant, and delicious for all adults.

13 ounces of any bitter or dark chocolate, chopped
2 tablespoons unsalted butter, diced
1 large egg yolk
1 ½ cups heavy cream, chilled
4 tablespoons granulated sugar
1 teaspoon vanilla extract
1 tablespoon Amaretto liquor

1. In a heatproof bowl, place the chopped chocolate and diced butter over a pot of simmering water. Stir until melted.
2. Then, whisk in the egg yolks vigorously and set aside.
3. In a stand mixer fitted with a paddle attachment, whip the very cold heavy cream, sugar, vanilla, and amaretto until stiff peaks.
4. Lastly, add the chocolate mixture to the cream mixture and whip on high for 2 minutes or until thick and incorporated.
5. Lastly, spoon or pipe the chocolate mousse into the prepared serving dishes using a pastry bag fitted with a fancy piping tip. Serve immediately or tightly wrap with plastic and store in the refrigerator before serving.

CREATIVE CANNOLI CREPE CAKE WITH CHERRY SAUCE

Serves 10 to 13

As an Italian, I was inspired to make this amazing cake when I saw the already made crepes at my local grocery store. As these crepes are very easy to find at any local grocery store, I decided it would be the perfect unique dessert to share with others. The addictively easy crepe cake is filled with a traditional cannoli filling and topped with cherry sauce, which is certain to catch anyone's eye.

Crepes
2 packages of ready-to-use crepes from your local grocery store (20 crepes)

Cannoli Filling
2 cups Ricotta cheese
a splash of whole milk
¾ cup powdered sugar
¼ cup heavy cream
Amaretto liquor to taste
½ cup semisweet chocolate shavings

1. In a stand mixer fitted with a whisk attachment, whip the cream on high speed until medium-stiff peaks form.
2. Then, with the mixer on slow, add the rest of the ingredients except for the chocolate shavings and continue to stir for 1 minute.
3. With the mixer turned off, use a spatula to fold the chocolate shavings into the cannoli filling. Set aside in the refrigerator before assembling.

Cherry Sauce
1 cup frozen sweet dark cherries, pitted
¼ cup granulated sugar
juice of ½ lemon
¼ cup water
1 tablespoon of cornstarch

1. Assemble the crepes on the serving plate of your choice.
2. Spread a heaping tablespoon of the cannoli crème on each of the crepes (20 individual crepes).
3. Stack the crepe on top of the cannoli crème and repeat the process until you have reached the last crepe. Refrigerate before serving.
4. For the cherry sauce, combine the frozen cherries, sugar, water, lemon juice, and cornstarch in a small saucepan and allow the sauce to come to a simmer until fully thickened (5 minutes). Cool before serving with the cake.
5. Just before serving, pour the cooled cherry sauce on top of the crepe cake or use it as a delicious side sauce.

AFFOGATO

Serves 6

Affogato is an Italian dessert that consists of a shot of espresso poured over a scoop of gelato. Warm espresso coffee with a scoop of your favorite gelato and toppings is bound to be a grand finale after any meal. This dessert couldn't be simpler as the espresso is prepped before the guests arrive and is heated and prepared right before serving. Creamy, warm, and satisfying.

---

1 cup boiling water
2 tablespoons espresso powder
6 tablespoons heavy cream, cold
1 pint of vanilla bean gelato (your choice: caramel, chocolate, coffee)
½ cup chocolate sauce
3 biscotti cookies, crumbled

1. Before serving, scoop the gelato in each of the 6 cups.
2. If you do not have an espresso maker that can make 6 shots of espresso, then stir the espresso powder and boiling water together until the powder dissolves.
3. Then, pour over the scooped gelato.
4. Then, pour a tablespoon of heavy cream between the 6 cups.
5. Lastly, drizzle with chocolate sauce and top with crushed biscotti cookies. Serve immediately.

TRADITIONAL RICE PUDDING

Serves 6 to 8
This Traditional Rice Pudding has been the common midnight snack in my family. My mother's recipe of Traditional Rice Pudding has been handed down to me where I have added one extra ingredient—rum. Warm, silky, creamy, sweet, and bursting with simple holiday flavors. Enjoy this magnificent one-pot dessert.

½ cup raisins (golden or dark)
1/3 cup rum
1 cup white grain rice
2 cups water
2 cups whole milk
3 tablespoons heavy cream
1 tablespoon unsalted butter
pinch of salt
8 ounces sweetened condensed milk
1 teaspoon ground cinnamon
pinch of ground nutmeg
½ tablespoon vanilla extract
1 large egg

1. In a small bowl combine the raisins and rum together and set aside until the rice pudding is fully cooked.
2. In a large pot, combine the rice, water, milk, cream, butter, and salt together. Bring to a boil and then reduce the heat to simmer with a lid over the top for 20 to 25 minutes. Stir occasionally. (The rice should be cooked at this time, but should still look creamy with liquid.)
3. Remove the pot from the heat and stir in the condensed milk, cinnamon, nutmeg, vanilla, and raisins that have absorbed the rum. (Drain any extra rum from the raisins unless you prefer extra.)
4. Place the pot over the stove for 3 to 5 more minutes to finish cooking.
5. Remove the pot from the stove and quickly whisk in the egg. Allow to cool slightly before serving.
•   If you do not have sweetened condensed milk, place a saucepan filled with 1 cup of heavy cream and 1 cup of sugar to a boil for 2 minutes. Add to the rice pudding along with the rest of the liquid and continue to cook.

VANILLA BEAN TRUFFLES

Makes 2 dozens of small truffles or 1 dozen large truffles.

This Vanilla Bean Truffle recipe is the perfect combination of sweet and bitter as these truffles are not too sugary. These truffles start with a white chocolate vanilla bean infused ganache that is hand rolled in a bitter dark chocolate. The combination of the white chocolate ganache along with the dark chocolate shell create a vanilla bean milk chocolate truffle, which couldn't be more divine and easy to make. These chocolate hand rolled truffles are not only incredibly fun to make with children and adults, but are also very simple. Enjoy this delicious, fun, and easy truffle recipe.

Vanilla White Chocolate Ganache
½ vanilla bean, scraped
¼ cup heavy cream
1 cup good quality white chocolate (Ghirardelli), chopped

- Prepare a baking sheet lined with parchment paper.
1. In a small saucepan over medium heat, boil the cream and vanilla bean that has been scraped and mixed. Remove the saucepan from the heat and allow to steep for 10 minutes.
2. Heat the cream and vanilla mixture over the stove again on medium heat until it comes to a simmer.
3. Pour over the chopped white chocolate and continue to stir until fully melted. Place the bowl in the refrigerator for 45 minutes or until the chocolate is set and hard.
4. Using a small ice cream or small spoon, roll the white chocolate in your hands, forming a circle, and place on a baking sheet lined with parchment paper. Place the truffles in the refrigerator while melting the dark chocolate.

Chocolate Shell
½ cup good quality bitter dark chocolate (Ghirardelli), chopped for coating

1. Place 1/3 of the chopped chocolate in a heatproof bowl over a pot of simmering water. Continue to stir until the chocolate is fully melted. Allow to cool slightly for 6 minutes.
2. Then, add the rest of the chopped chocolate and continue to stir until melted.
3. Then, using the palm of your hands, scoop a spoonful of the melted dark chocolate in your hand while rolling the white chocolate truffle in it. Continue this until all truffles have been rolled in the dark chocolate.
4. Lastly, place the truffles in the refrigerator for 15 minutes to set before serving.

LIGHT AND BRIGHT STRAWBERRY PARFAIT

Serves 4

This bright and light dessert is an elegant and delicious treat. Serve this mouthwatering treat to children, family members, or even at special events as you can make these two components ahead of time and assemble later. This dessert first starts with the whip cream–mascarpone mixture, which is sweetened with vanilla and lemon zest. The rest of the beautiful layers consist of fresh strawberries mixed with lemon juice and sprinkled with crisp meringue cookies. Creamy and velvety, sweet, but refreshing, and lastly, crunchily rewarding.

Mascarpone Cream Mixture
1 cup heavy whipping cream
¼ cup granulated sugar
1 teaspoon vanilla extract
½ teaspoon lemon zest
½ cup mascarpone, softened

• Have four small glass cups or mini trifle dishes ready to assemble.
1. In a stand mixer fitted with a whisk attachment, whip the heavy cream, sugar, vanilla, and lemon zest together until soft peaks form.
2. Then, turn off the mixer and add the softened mascarpone and whip on high speed just until it comes together (30 seconds). Turn off mixer and set aside in the refrigerator.

Strawberry Layer
2 cups strawberries, cut into quarters
juice from ½ lemon
4 large meringue cookies, 2 roughly chopped and 2 cut in half

1. In a bowl, mix the cut strawberries and lemon juice.
2. Then, cut 2 meringue cookies in half to top for decoration and roughly chop the last 2 to sprinkle over the strawberries.
3. Lastly, scoop a heavy dollop of the cream mixture at the bottom of the cups. Then, add some strawberries and their juice. Lastly, sprinkle over the meringue cookies. Repeat these steps until all glasses are full and topped with the last half of the meringue cookie for decoration.

GRANDMA JULIAN'S FAMOUS RASPBERRY JELL-O DESSERT

Serves 12 to 14

My grandmother's raspberry Jell-O dessert has been in the family for years. This dish satisfies all of the textures needed in all dessert as it is fruity sweet, tangy, creamy, and crunchy. It may seem untraditional or different when you first hear it, but I promise it will be loved and asked about by everyone. This is the one dessert we will always have at every family gathering. This dish can be left in the refrigerator for days as it will only develop better flavors. Enjoy!

Raspberry Jell-O
1 6-ounce raspberry Jell-O
2 ½ cups hot water
1 small 7-ounce apple sauce
1 12-ounce pack frozen raspberries, thawed
½ cup granulated sugar

1. In the 9x13 or any trifle dish of your choice, dissolve the raspberry Jell-O and hot water, whisking constantly until the powder dissolves.
2. Stir in the applesauce, thawed raspberries, and sugar together.
3. Allow to sit in the refrigerator for at least 1 hour or even overnight if needed.

Sour Cream Topping
1-pound sour cream (You may add less if you want a thinner layer of sour cream.)
1 cup chopped walnuts

1. Once the Jell-O has set and you are ready to ice, spread the sour cream over the Jell-O using a knife or spoon.
2. Lastly, sprinkle over the chopped walnuts. Keep in the refrigerator before serving.

TROPICAL GRILLED PINEAPPLE WITH COCONUT SORBET

Serves 4

Bring the Bahamas to your home with this juicy and refreshing dessert. This dessert couldn't be easier and quicker to make. Fresh cut pineapple grilled outside or on the stovetop is drenched in a brown sugar/rum glaze and then topped off with coconut sorbet. This dessert is timeless and even more satisfying when enjoyed with family and friends.

Sliced Pineapple
1 small fresh pineapple, trimmed and sliced into 4 circles

Brown Sugar Glaze
½ cup water
½ cup brown sugar
splash of rum
¼ cup granulated sugar for sprinkling

Coconut Sorbet
4 scoops coconut sorbet (store-bought 1 pint)

1. In a small saucepan, stir together the water, brown sugar, and rum.
2. Allow to simmer over medium high heat for 2 minutes. Then, turn off the heat.
3. Take the sliced pineapple and dip in the warm syrup for 1 minute.
4. Allow the excess syrup to drip off the pineapple and place on a preheated grill (either stove top or BBQ).
5. Sprinkle both sides of the pineapple with sugar and grill on medium high heat on each side for 2 minutes or until golden brown grill marks appear.
6. Serve warm with a scoop of coconut sorbet on top.

STUNNING SAUTÉED CINNAMON APPLES

Serves 4 to 6

My recipe of Sautéed Cinnamon Apples is the simplest and most indulging dessert anyone could make. The juicy Granny Smith apples along with their warm juice that is infused with butter and cinnamon will leave you cuddling up by the fire. This quick-to-make dessert is best served warm by itself or with a scoop of ice cream and whip cream or even your oatmeal. Enjoy this recipe all times of the year as it can be made weeks or even months in advanced if stored properly in the freezer and warmed through before serving.

2 Granny Smith apples, peeled, cored, cut ¼ inch thick
4 tablespoons unsalted butter, melted
½ tablespoon ground cinnamon
½ cup brown sugar
2 tablespoons granulated sugar
juice of 1 lemon
pinch of salt
splash of water or lemon juice, if needed

1. In a saucepan, melt the butter until it reaches a medium brown color.
2. With the pan very hot, add the cut apples, cinnamon, sugars, lemon juice, and salt together.
3. Stir and cook over medium heat for 2 minutes. (If the apples look too dry and there is not enough juice, then add a splash of water or lemon juice.)
4. Reduce the heat to low and put a lid on the saucepan for 5 to 6 minutes or until apples have softened and the juice has slightly thickened.
5. Serve warm over ice cream, whip cream, or frozen yogurt.

EFFORTLESS NO-CHURN ICE CREAM

Makes 1 ½ quarts

My recipes for No-Churn Ice Cream will have you amazed at how simple and delicious these ice creams can be. I am providing 3 different types of ice cream flavors that all have 5 or less ingredients. It first starts out with a simple ice cream base, and to that, you may add any ingredients to flavor the ice cream. Some ideas would be to add caramel sauce to make caramel ice cream or almond and marsh-mallows in a chocolate ice cream base to make rocky road ice cream. As you can see, this recipe will become your most loved as you can transform any ice cream to healthy and fruity or sweet and sugary.

Ice Cream Base
1 14-ounce can of condensed milk
1 pint or ½-quart heavy cream
pinch of salt

- Have a large 1-quart container for your ice cream to freeze in.
1. In a stand mixer fitted with a paddle attachment, whip the cream starting on low speed.
2. Once the cream has reached soft peaks, drizzle in the condensed milk and pinch of salt.
3. Continue to whip for 1 more minute and then turn the mixer off.
4. Place the ice cream in the container and freeze until completely firm.

Strawberry Ice Cream
¾ cup good quality strawberry jam
¾ cup fresh strawberries, cut into quarters

1. Once the ice cream base is finished, quickly whisk in the jam and strawberries.

Vanilla Ice Cream
½ tablespoon vanilla extract or 1 vanilla bean, scraped

1. Once the ice cream base is finished, quickly whisk in the vanilla extract or scraped vanilla bean.

Chocolate Ice Cream
¼ Special Dark Hershey's Cocoa Powder
½ cup chocolate syrup, to drizzle

1. Once the ice cream base is finished, quickly whisk in the cocoa powder and drizzle with chocolate syrup in the ice cream and on top.

FUN FRIED BANANA SPLIT

Serves 4

If you thought banana split was amazing, imagine fried banana split! Semi-ripe bananas
dipped in a light funnel cake batter and fried for only 3 minutes, which is then topped with
ice cream and crunchy toppings. You could also make the fried bananas ahead of time and
keep in a warm oven. This last-minute indulgent dessert will be your next favorite treat.

Fried Banana
4 semi-ripe Bananas
3 cups vegetable oil, for frying
2 large eggs
¼ cup granulated sugar
1 cup whole milk
1 1/3 Cup all-purpose flour
1 teaspoon baking powder
¼ teaspoon salt
½ tablespoon vanilla extract
½ cup powdered sugar, for dusting

- Fill a medium-sized pot with the 3 cups of vegetable oil or fill the pot 1/3 of the way up and heat to 325 degrees on medium-high heat. Check the temperature with a candy thermometer.
1. While the oil is heating, prepare the batter for the bananas. In a mixing bowl, whisk all of the ingredients together.
2. Peel the bananas and dip each banana completely in the batter.
3. Carefully, place the banana in the heated oil and allow to cook for 1 ½ minutes on each side or until golden brown. Continue until you have finished all 4 bananas.
4. Place the cooked bananas on a plate or paper towel to drain the excess oil and dust with powdered sugar.

Ice Cream and Toppings
3 different flavors of ice cream (my choice: chocolate, vanilla, and caramel)
½ cup chocolate sauce
½ cup prepared caramel sauce
1 cup prepared whip cream
1/3 cup sweetened coconut flakes
½ cup toasted almonds
1/3 cup rainbow sprinkles
4 Maraschino cherries

1. While the bananas are still hot, scoop the different flavored ice creams and add the rest of the toppings. Serve immediately.

FRUITY PEBBLE KID'S TREATS

Serves 6

My fun Fruity Pebble Kid's Treats was inspired one day while I was baking for an eight-year-old's birthday party. These treats are a cute spin on rice krispes and can even be mixed in with normal rice krispes for a fruity flavor. These treats are bright, fun, and delicious as they can be used to make with children and shared with everyone.

3 tablespoons unsalted butter
4 cups large marshmallows or 110-ounce bag
1 teaspoon vanilla extract
6 ½ Cups Rice Krispe Fruity Pebbles

- In a large bowl, measure the fruity pebbles and set aside.
1. In a small saucepan, melt the butter and then add the marshmallows.
2. Continue to stir until the marshmallows have melted and then turn off the heat.
3. Stir in the vanilla and then pour over the fruit pebbles. Gently mix until combined.
4. Place the fruity pebble mixture on a nonstick 4x4 baking sheet and press gently with damp fingers.
5. Place in the refrigerator for at least one hour or even overnight.
6. Cut into adorable shapes using cookie cutters or a knife and serve.

♦ Keep in the refrigerator if making ahead of time.

THE HOT CHOCOLATE

Serves 4

My Hot Chocolate is known by many to not only be the easiest, but the most decadent. It is not thick and overly rich. It is perfectly light, smooth, and chocolaty. The secret ingredient is the Hershey's Special Dark Cocoa powder. Stir in a small amount of the cocoa powder with any of your favorite hot chocolate powder mix and add milk and half-and-half. Lastly, top with whip cream and you will immediately have perfection. Perfect, simple, and indulging.

Hot Chocolate
3 cups whole milk
½ cup+ 1 tablespoon Nesquik chocolate milk powder (brand of your choice)
3 tablespoons Hershey's Special Dark Cocoa powder

1. In a medium-sized saucepan, heat the milk and half-and-half over medium heat.
2. Once warm, whisk in the chocolate powder and cocoa powder. Turn off the heat when heated to your preference.
3. Continue to whisk until there are no more lumps. Serve immediately.

Fresh Whip Cream
1 cup heavy whipping cream
3 tablespoons confectioner's sugar
1 teaspoon vanilla extract

1. In a stand mixer fitted with a whisk attachment, whip the heavy cream, sugar, and vanilla extract starting on low speed and gradually increase the speed.
2. Turn off the mixer when the whip cream has come to stiff peaks and completely thickened.
3. Dollop on top of the hot chocolate.

Cookies

TRADITIONAL CHOCOLATE CHIP COOKIES

Makes 1 dozen of medium-sized cookies
My chocolate chip cookie recipe has been perfected over a period of years. I have tried many different ingredients and recently came across my most loved. These cookies are thin, but chewy with the best buttery flavor, along with the most important flavors of vanilla and chocolate. Adding a small amount of molasses will heighten the cookie's flavor, making it taste rich and decadent. Indulge in the most delicious chocolate chip cookie ever.

½ cup + 2 tablespoons packed brown sugar
½ cup granulated sugar
12 tablespoons or 1 ½ stick unsalted butter
1 large egg
1 ½ teaspoon vanilla extract
2 teaspoons unsulfured molasses (If you do not have molasses, add extra vanilla.)
1 ½ cup + 2 tablespoons all-purpose flour
1 teaspoon salt
½ teaspoon baking soda
1 ¼ cup semisweet chocolate chips or chunks

- Preheat the oven to 325 degrees and place a sheet of parchment paper on 2 large baking sheets.
1. In a stand mixer fitted with a paddle attachment, beat the butter, sugar, molasses, and vanilla together for 2 minutes.
2. Add the egg and beat until fully incorporated. Turn off the mixer and scrape down the bowl.
3. Add the dry ingredients and stir until combined.
4. Lastly, fold in the chocolate chips.
5. Scoop the chocolate chip batter using a medium-sized ice cream scoop and leave plenty of room for the cookies to spread during baking.
6. Refrigerate for 30 minutes or freeze for weeks.
7. Before baking, allow to come to room temperature and bake for 13 to 14 minutes.

CHEWY OATMEAL RAISIN COOKIES

Makes 1 dozen medium-sized cookies

My deliciously sweet oatmeal raisin cookie recipe uses the same ingredients as the chocolate chip, but it has a few extra elements: ground cinnamon, sweet dark raisins, and chewy oats make this cookie sweet, hardy, and filling. Your grandparents will say it tastes just like their childhood. Treat yourself to a cookie you will be making and sharing with others all year round.

---

12 tablespoons or 1 ½ stick unsalted butter
½ cup + 2 tablespoons packed brown sugar
½ cup granulated sugar
1 large egg
1 ½ teaspoon vanilla extract
2 teaspoons unsulfured molasses (If you do not have molasses, add extra vanilla.)
1 ½ cup + 2 tablespoons all-purpose flour
1 teaspoon salt
½ teaspoon baking soda
1 teaspoon ground cinnamon
¾ cup dark Raisins
1 ½ cups old-fashioned rolled oats

- Preheat the oven to 325 degrees and place a sheet of parchment paper on 2 large baking sheets.
1. In a stand mixer fitted with a paddle attachment, beat the butter, sugars, molasses, and vanilla together for 2 minutes.
2. Add the egg and beat until fully incorporated. Turn off the mixer and scrape down the bowl.
3. Add the dry ingredients and stir until combined.
4. Lastly, fold in the raisins and oats.
5. Scoop the oatmeal raisin batter using a medium-sized ice cream scoop and leave plenty of room for the cookies to spread during baking.
6. Refrigerate for 30 minutes or freeze for weeks.
7. Before baking, allow the dough to come to room temperature and bake for 13 to 14 minutes.

MAMA'S EVERYTHING BUT THE KITCHEN SINK

Makes 1 dozen medium-sized cookies

My amazing Mama's Everything but the Kitchen Sink cookies are famous in our household. Although I do not make them as often as I want to, they remind everyone of my beautiful mother when I share the cookies with others. These deliciously chewy cookies have tremendous flavor as they have many high quality ingredients. These cookies contain coconut, walnuts, chocolate chips, pretzels, oats, and toffee bits. Have fun with these insanely tasty cookies.

12 tablespoons or 1 ½ stick unsalted butter

½ cup + 2 tablespoons packed brown sugar

½ cup granulated sugar

1 large egg

1 ½ teaspoon vanilla extract

2 teaspoons unsulfured molasses

1 ½ cup + 2 tablespoons all-purpose flour

1 teaspoon salt

½ teaspoon baking soda

1 ½ cups old-fashioned rolled oats

¾ cup sweetened shredded coconut

1 cup chocolate chunks

½ cup broken pretzels

½ cup chopped walnuts

½ cup chopped Almond Roca or Toffee Bits

• Preheat the oven to 325 degrees and place a sheet of parchment paper on 2 large baking sheets.

1. In a stand mixer fitted with a paddle attachment, beat the butter, sugars, molasses, and vanilla together for 2 minutes.

2. Add the egg and beat until fully incorporated. Turn off the mixer and scrape down the bowl.

3. Add the dry ingredients and stir until combined.

4. Lastly, fold in rolled oats, coconut, chocolate chips, pretzels, walnuts, and the chopped Almond Roca.

5. Scoop the cookie batter using a medium-sized ice cream scoop and leave plenty of room for the cookies to spread during baking.

6. Refrigerate for 30 minutes or freeze for weeks.

7. Before baking, allow the dough to come to room temperature and bake for 13 to 14 minutes.

◆ If you do not have molasses, then you may add extra vanilla extract.

NO-FAIL SUGAR/SHORTBREAD COOKIES

Makes 1 dozen cookies depending on cookie cutter size

I promise you, you will be thanking me later for this amazing and no-fail cookie recipe. These cookies are a mix between a sugar and shortbread cookie because they contain a lot of butter, but they are incredibly soft and flavorful as they contain almond and vanilla extract. It is the almond extract that leaves everyone so happy they tried this cookie. Stamp these cookies with any cookie cutter and bake immediately. Decorate with chocolate, royal icing or frosting for special events. *But* the beautiful thing is that these cookies don't have to have any toppings. They are delicious just by themselves. You're welcome!

1 cup unsalted butter, softened
1 cup granulated sugar
½ tablespoon almond extract
½ tablespoon vanilla extract
1 large egg
3 cups all-purpose flour
2 teaspoons baking powder
pinch of salt

- Preheat the oven to 350 degrees and place parchment paper on 2 large baking sheets.
1. In a stand mixer fitted with the paddle attachment, beat the butter, sugar, and extracts together for 2 minutes.
2. Then, add the eggs and beat until combined. Scrape down the bowl.
3. Lastly, add the dry ingredients and stir until it almost comes together.
4. Dump the dough on a floured surface and roll out to ½ inch thick.
5. Stamp the cookies using a medium-sized cookie cutter. (Use bigger cookie cutters for smaller amounts.)
6. Place the cookies on a baking sheet and bake for 8 to 13 minutes or until slightly firm to the touch and not golden brown. (Depending on baking sheet, the cookies may slightly brown on the bottoms which is fine.)
7. Decorate with melted chocolate, royal icing, frosting, or nothing.

Royal Icing

4 cups confectioner's sugar
3 large egg whites
squirt of lemon
1 teaspoon vanilla extract

1. In a stand mixer fitted with the whisk attachment, whip all of the ingredients together for 2 minutes. (The lemon makes the icing very white.)
2. Color the icing or leave as is.
3. Using a spoon or paintbrush, ice the cookies.

SWEET-FILLED COOKIES

Makes 1 dozen medium-sized cookies

Sweet-Filled Cookies are a sugar/shortbread mixed cookie that contain any jam, jelly, or sweet filling you could imagine. This cookie uses the recipe from the previous page of No-Fail Sugar/Shortbread Cookie. Since these cookies are flavorful and soft, they can standup to any sweet and luscious filling. Some ideas would be fruity jams or jellies for holidays, chocolate ganache for events, and frostings for kids. I know you'll enjoy these adorable Sweet-Filled Cookies

---

Sugar/Shortbread Cookie Dough

1 cup unsalted butter, softened
1 cup granulated sugar
½ tablespoon almond extract
½ tablespoon vanilla extract
1 large egg
3 cups all-purpose flour
2 teaspoons baking powder
pinch of salt

- Preheat the oven to 350 degrees and place parchment paper on 2 large baking sheets.
1. In a stand mixer fitted with the paddle attachment, beat the butter, sugar, and extracts together for 2 minutes.
2. Then, add the eggs and beat until combined. Scrape down the bowl.
3. Lastly, add the dry ingredients and stir until it almost comes together.
4. Dump the dough on a floured surface and roll out to ½ inch thick.
5. Stamp the cookie dough using a small cookie cutter.
6. After stamping all the cookie dough, go back to stamp half of the cookies in the center of the dough using a very small cookie cutter (these are the lids).
7. Place the cookies on a baking sheet and bake for 8 to 13 minutes or until slightly firm to the touch and not golden brown. (Depending on baking sheet, the cookies may slightly brown on the bottoms which is fine.)

Sweet-Filling Choices

½ cup raspberry jam
½ cup strawberry jelly
½ cup Nutella
½ cup ganache

1. After the cookies have baked and cooled, take the cookies that have not been stamped in the middle and fill with any filling of your choice. Make sure to leave a small border around the edges so the filling does not spill of the cookie.
2. Lastly, place the lid (the cookie that was stamped in the middle) on the sweet-filled cookie and store in the refrigerator or eat immediately.

OMG GINGER MOLASSES COOKIES

Makes 2 dozens of medium-sized cookies

My OMG Ginger Molasses Cookies will be devoured by everyone in seconds. I yielded this recipe to make 2 dozens because you will want to share 1 dozen and eat the other dozen. These cookies are moist, sweet, flavorful, and gorgeous since they have dark molasses, ginger, and vanilla inside them. These flavors imitate holiday ingredients, but I promise you people will be begging for them all year round.

2 ¼ sticks unsalted butter, softened
2 ½ cups granulated sugar
3 large eggs
¾ cup dark molasses
1 teaspoon vanilla extract
8 cups all-purpose flour
1 ½ teaspoon baking soda
1 teaspoon salt
1 tablespoon cinnamon
1 tablespoon cloves
1 tablespoon ground ginger
1 cup granulated sugar, for rolling

- Preheat the oven to 350 degrees and place parchment paper on 2 large baking sheets.
1. In a stand mixer fitted with a paddle attachment, beat the butter and sugar together for 2 minutes.
2. Add the eggs and continue to beat for 1 minute.
3. Then, add the molasses and beat until combined.
4. Lastly, add the dry ingredients and scrape down the bowl.
5. Refrigerate the dough for 30 minutes.
6. Once chilled, scoop the dough using an ice cream scoop and roll the cookies in the granulated sugar. Leave plenty of space between the cookies as they will spread. Bake for 10 to 12 minutes.

SUPER CUTE SPRINKLE COOKIES

Makes 2 dozen of medium- to small-sized cookies

My deliciously soft and fun Sprinkle Cookies are a hit at any themed event. These cookies are perfect for a special treat for your children and of course yourself. Customize these cookies by decorating with any colored sprinkles you have in your pantry. These soft buttery cookies are rolled in the palm of your hand and then transferred to a dish of colorful sprinkles that are then baked off. Choose green and red sprinkles for the holidays or blue and red sprinkles for the Fourth of July! Enjoy!

---

12 tablespoon unsalted butter, softened
¾ cup granulated sugar
1 large egg
2 teaspoons vanilla extract
½ teaspoons almond extract
zest ½ lemon
1 ½ cup all-purpose flour
1 ½ teaspoon baking powder
½ teaspoon salt
1 cup colored sprinkles

- Preheat the oven to 325 degrees and place parchment paper on 3 baking sheets.
1. In a stand mixer fitted with a paddle attachment, beat the butter and sugar together for 2 minutes.
2. Add the egg, vanilla, almond, and lemon zest into the stand mixer and continue to stir until fully combined. Scrape down the bowl.
3. Lastly, add the dry ingredients on low speed until combined.
4. Scoop the dough using a medium-sized ice cream scoop and roll in the palms of your hands to form a ball. Then, roll the dough balls in the sprinkles until the ball is completely coated with colorful sprinkles.
5. Flatten slightly to form a disk and refrigerate the dough for 30 minutes on a baking sheet.
6. Remove the baking sheet from the refrigerator and bake for 10 to 12 minutes or until lightly browned on the bottom.

DOUBLE CHOCOLATE FUDGE CRINKLE COOKIES

Makes 1 dozen medium-sized cookies

These Double Chocolate Fudge Crinkle Cookies will become your most loved chocolate cookie. These chocolate fudge cookies are moist, but chewy, and lastly sweet and indulgent. My recipe requires a high-grade semisweet baking chocolate that is then baked off and rolled in powdered sugar so when the cookies are done, they have a divine whimsical presentation. Treat yourself to a chocolate cookie lovers' dream!

2 cups semisweet baking chocolate, chopped and melted
3 tablespoons unsalted butter, melted
3 large eggs
½ cup granulated sugar
½ teaspoon vanilla extract
¾ cup all-purpose flour
¼ teaspoon baking powder
1 cup powdered sugar

- Preheat the oven to 350 degrees and place parchment paper on 2 baking sheets.
1. In a heatproof bowl over simmering water, melt the chopped chocolate and butter together. Once melted, take off the heat and set aside.
2. In a separate bowl, whisk together the egg, sugar, and vanilla extract together.
3. Add the melted chocolate mixture to the egg and sugar and continue to whisk until incorporated.
4. Lastly, add the dry ingredients and stir until combined.
5. Then, place the cookie dough in the refrigerator for 30 minutes.
6. Scoop the cookie dough using a medium-sized ice cream scoop and roll each ball in the powdered sugar. Press down slightly on the cookie dough and place on a baking sheet.
7. Bake for 12 to 14 minutes or until slightly firm on the corners.

DELECTABLE COCONUT MACAROON COOKIES

Makes 1 dozen cookies

My Delectable Coconut Macaroon Cookies are the best coconut macaroons in the world because of their rich flavor and moist texture! My cookies are so delectable because not only do they contain sweetened flakey coconut, but also they have silky sweetened condensed milk and rich cream cheese. It is the combination of the cream cheese and sweetened condensed milk that makes these cookies so moist and sticky. Enjoy these cookies with a cup of coffee or tea!

1 14-ounce package shredded sweetened coconut
1 14-ounce can sweetened condensed milk
1/3 cup cream cheese, softened
1 teaspoon vanilla extract
2 large egg whites
pinch of salt

- Preheat the oven to 325 degrees and place parchment paper on 2 large baking sheets.
1. In a stand mixer fitted with a whisk attachment, whip the egg whites and salt until firm peaks.
2. While the egg whites are whipping, mix together the coconut, condensed milk, cream cheese, and vanilla using a fork to break up the room-temperature cream cheese.
3. Once the egg whites have whipped to firm peaks, turn off the mixer and using a spatula, fold ½ off the egg whites into the coconut mixture until combined. Repeat this step with the last half of egg whites.
4. Refrigerate the dough for 30 minutes.
5. Scoop the chilled dough using a medium sized ice cream scoop and place on a baking sheet. Bake for 24 to 25 minutes or until golden brown.

VANILLA MADELINE COOKIES

Makes 16 normal-sized Madeline cookies

My fantastic Vanilla Madeline Cookies are moist, flavorful, and will be loved by all. These elegant and sophisticated cookies are not only delightful, but also perfect for large crowds as they can be saved in the refrigerator or freezer for weeks. Even though these cookies require a few extra steps, this recipe will be the easiest you will ever find. Whip eggs, sugar, vanilla, and lemon together until light and airy while folding in the dry ingredients and the luscious melted butter. Fill a Madeline mold with the luscious batter and bake. Be ready to be amazed by my adorable Vanilla Madeline Cookies!

3 large eggs
½ cup granulated sugar
1 ½ tablespoon dark brown sugar
1 ½ teaspoon vanilla extract
½ teaspoon lemon zest
1 cup all-purpose flour
½ teaspoon baking powder
pinch of salt
1 stick unsalted butter, melted
½ cup confectioner's sugar, for dusting

- Preheat the oven to 350 degrees and grease a Madeline pan liberally.
1. In a saucepan, melt the butter over medium low heat. Set aside.
2. In a stand mixer fitted with a whisk attachment, whip the eggs, sugar, brown sugar, vanilla, and lemon zest together for 8 to 10 minutes or until thickened and pale in color.
3. Then, fold the dry ingredients into the egg mixture in 2 additions.
4. Lastly, gently whisk in the melted butter until incorporated.
5. Refrigerate covered for at least 1 hour.
6. Once chilled, fill a piping bag in order to fill the molds three-quarters of the way up. (These molds could be anything. I used a shell mold).
7. Bake for 8 to 12 minutes or until completely baked.
8. Use an offset spatula or knife to lift the cookies out of the mold immediately and dust with powdered sugar.

TOASTED S'MORE COOKIES

Makes 1 dozen medium sized cookies

My recipe for Toasted S'more cookies couldn't be easier and more fun as they are perfect for any event and can be made days in advanced. These cookies are a chocolate chip cookie base that is filled with rich chocolate ganache, toasted marshmallow, and crumbled graham crackers. It is basically a toasted s'more cookie sandwich…Yum! Have fun with these must have cookies!

12 Tablespoons or 1 ½ Stick Unsalted Butter, room temperature
½ Cup+ 2 Tablespoon Packed Brown Sugar
½ Granulated Sugar
1 Large Egg
1 ½ teaspoon Vanilla Extract
2 teaspoons Unsulfured Molasses (if you do not have molasses, add extra Vanilla)

1 ½ Cup + 2 tablespoon All-Purpose Flour
1 teaspoon Salt
½ teaspoon Baking Soda
1 ¼ Cup Ghirardelli Dark Chocolate Chips
3 Graham Crackers, Crushed
12 Large Marshmallows

- Preheat the oven to 350 degrees and place parchment paper on 2 large baking sheets.
1. In a stand mixer fitted with a paddle attachment, beat the butter and sugars together for two minutes.
2. Add the egg and beat until fully incorporated. Turn off the mixer and scrape down the bowl.
3. Add the dry ingredients and stir until combined.
4. Lastly, fold in the chocolate chips.
5. Scoop the chocolate chip batter using a medium sized ice cream scoop and leave plenty of room for the cookies to spread during baking.
6. Refrigerate for 30 minutes or freeze for weeks.
7. Before baking, allow to come to room temperature and bake for 13 to 15 minutes.
8. Remove the pan from the oven and allow to cool completely before assembling.

Chocolate Ganache

2 cups Semi-Sweet Chocolate Chips
1 Cup Heavy Cream, Hot

- Heat the heavy cream in a small saucepan.
1. Before the heavy cream comes to a simmer, poor the cream over the chocolate chips and continue to stir until fully melted.
2. Set aside for 30 minutes before assembling the S'more Cookies.
3. Once the ganache has cooled, take one cookie and spoon the ganache over the top.
4. Then, add one large marshmallow and toast using a small crème Brule torcher.
5. Lastly, top with the second chocolate chip cookie.

Chocolate Dipped

CHOCOLATE DIPPED LEFTOVERS?

This trick of dipping leftover desserts in white, milk, or dark chocolate is genius. Many of these desserts can be saved in plastic wrap or foil and frozen for 1 to 2 months. When you are ready to enjoy your leftovers, allow them to come to room temperature and dip or drizzle in any type of chocolate. First, melt the chocolate in a double boiler over medium heat while stirring. Do not allow the chocolate to get too hot or it will burn. White chocolate contains mostly fat, so it will melt the quickest. Once the desserts are dipped, allow to set on a piece of parchment paper and transfer to the refrigerator for 2 minutes. Lastly, if you are dipping fruit in chocolate, I recommend that you do not store the chocolate dipped fruit in the refrigerator as it will sweet and look dissatisfying. Once you have dipped the fruit in the chocolate, set aside on a sheet of parchment paper and let it set in the refrigerator for 3 minutes. Then, remove the fruit from the refrigerator after 3 minutes and set aside until you are ready to enjoy. Enjoy my fun and helpful trick to amazingly delicious leftovers!

White Chocolate
Melt 1 cup of white chocolate over a double boiler of simmering water for 5 to 6 minutes.

Milk Chocolate
Melt 1 cup of milk chocolate over a double boiler of simmering water for 6 to 7 minutes.

Dark Chocolate
Melt 1 cup of dark chocolate over a double boiler of simmering water for 6 to 8 minutes.

Just too good!

ABOUT THE AUTHOR

As a fun, young, and creative entrepreneur, Nicci has devoted her hard work to the art of baking. Her appetite for creative work has allowed her to find new ways of having fun in the kitchen that can relate to every baker. She enjoys sharing knowledge of ingredients with others and is always willing to work any job she can. Even though she is a baker at heart, she enjoys studying business entrepreneurship and working special events.

As she experiments with new recipes that are tested on her own clients, she takes notes of what people enjoy the most. Then, she will create a creative, but enticing baking book that guarantees easy satisfaction.

Confectious was started in Nicci's home and still continues as she makes all custom cakes, pastries, and baked goods that are sold by word of mouth. She began her journey at a young age and carried it through all the way to the Culinary Institute of America, Greystone where she studied baking and pastry.

However, her urge for creativity and love for her family drove her back home where she could start her own business and still obtain her business degree close to home. Nicci's craving to bake anything addictively easy is what will allow her and *Confectious* to become so successful! This hungry girl will always keep you on your toes for new and delicious easy to make treats!

CPSIA information can be obtained at www.ICGtesting.com
Printed in the USA
BVOW07s2020200116

433658BV00023B/198/P

9 781682 138830